First published in Great Britain in 2001 by Andersen Press Ltd., 20 Vauxhall Bridge Road,
London SW1V 2SA. Published in Australia by Random House Australia Pty., 20 Alfred
Street, Milsons Point, Sydney, NSW 2061. All rights reserved. Colour separated in Italy by
Fotoriproduzioni Beverari, Verona. Printed and bound in Italy by Grafiche AZ, Verona.

10   9   8   7   6   5   4   3   2   1

British Library Cataloguing in Publication Data available.
ISBN 1 84270 001 4
This book has been printed on acid-free paper

We're all going on a summer holiday . . . sang Preston's mum and dad as they headed off for a week at the seaside.

I'm going, too!

"Just think of it," said Preston.
"Sunshine, sea, sand . . ."
". . . And sausages!"
said Mister Wolf.

At last they arrived.
During the journey, Preston
was only sick twice,

and he only said,
"Are we nearly there yet?"
thirty-seven times.

Preston slipped on his swimsuit,
slapped on his sunhat,
slopped on his sunscreen
and set off across the sand.
Suddenly!

"Why don't you look where
you're going?" said the little girl.
"Sorry," said Preston.
"Are you all right?"

"I suppose so," said the little
girl. "How about you?"
"My nose hurts," said Preston.

"What's your name?"
asked the little girl.
"Preston,"
said Preston.
"What's yours?"
"Maxine," said Maxine.
"But everyone calls me
Max. You're fat."
"Thank you," said Preston.
"You're rather plump yourself.
I like your swimsuit."
"Thank you," said Max,
and she gave
a little
twirl.

"How's your nose?" said Max.
"It hurts," said Preston.
"I'll kiss it better!" said Max.
And she did.

"You're blushing!" said Max.
"Must be sunburn," said Preston.
"You're funny," said Max.
"Let's play," said Preston.

The next day was Sunday . . .

Preston was up bright
and early to meet Max.
"Let's make sandcastles," said Max.
And they did. All day.

Max told Preston her dad was a lifeguard so she spent the whole summer on the beach. "Lucky you!" said Preston.

On Monday they went surfing . . .
"Wave!" shouted Max.
"Who to?"
shouted Preston.
"You goof!"
laughed Max –
"How's your nose?"
"Tender!"
shouted Preston.
"Kiss it better?"
shouted Max.
"Race you to
the beach!"
shouted Preston.

On Tuesday they dug a hole . . .

"How's your nose today?" said Max.
"Sore!" said Preston.
"Kiss it better?" said Max.
"Thank you, nurse!" said Preston.

On Wednesday they
explored rock pools . . .

"Watch out for the
slippery seaweed," said Max.
"Yes," giggled Preston.
"If I slipped I *might* hurt
my nose again . . ."
". . . and I *might* have to kiss it
better again!" giggled Max.

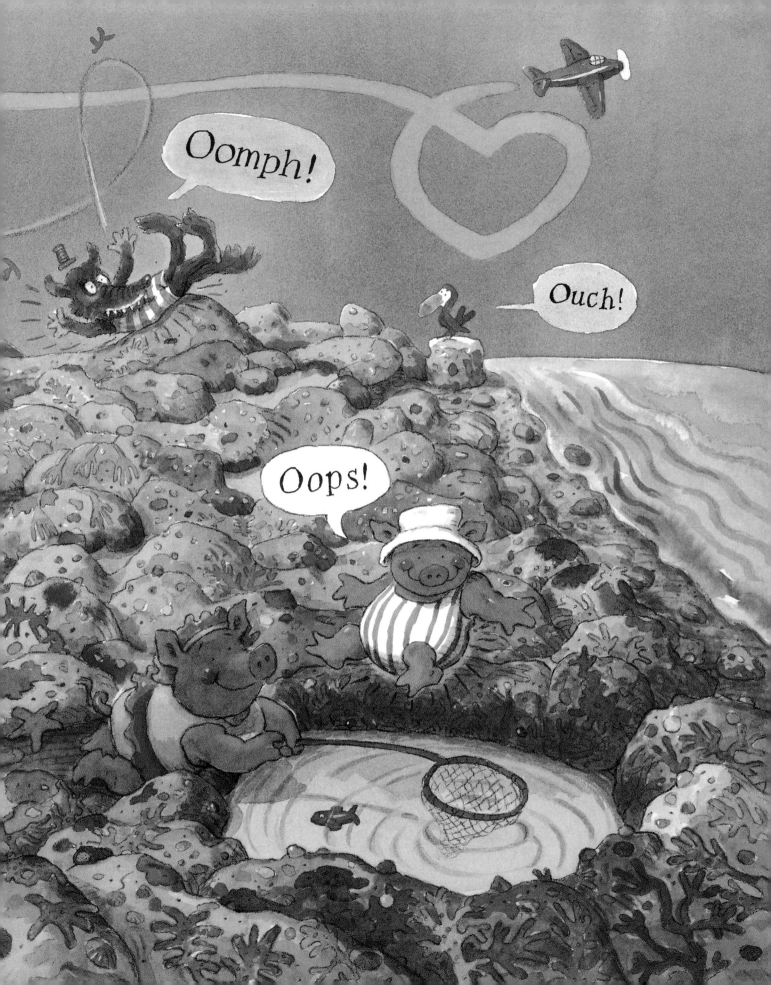

On Thursday they
went sailing . . .

"I hope you put plenty of
sun cream on your nose,"
said Max. "Otherwise . . ."
". . .You *might* have to kiss
it better!" laughed Preston.

On Friday they went snorkelling . . .

And on Saturday they said goodbye . . .

"Come back soon!"
shouted Max.
"Soon as I can!"
shouted Preston.
"Preston!" shouted Max.
"Did you know you had
a wolf on your roofrack?"
"Very funny!"
shouted Preston.
"Goodbye, Max.
I'll write
to you!"

'bye
Preston.

And this is what he wrote . . .

Dear Max,
I'm back home now
and my nose is
better, thanks to
you (blush blush).
I wish I was still
at the seaside
with you.
I had the best time
ever. Thank you for
being my friend.
I miss you.
Love Preston xxx